Queen Aurora's Birthday Surprise

Special thanks to
Elizabeth Galloway
For Neve Farrell

ORCHARD BOOKS

First published in Great Britain in 2020 by The Watts Publishing Group

1 3 5 7 9 10 8 6 4 2

A CIP catalogue record for this book is available from the British Library.

ISBN 978 1 40835 712 5

Printed and bound in Great Britain by Clays Ltd, Elcograf S.p.A.

The paper and board used in this book are made from wood from responsible sources.

Orchard Books
An imprint of Hachette Children's Group
Part of The Watts Publishing Group Limited
Carmelite House
50 Victoria Embankment
London EC4Y 0DZ

An Hachette UK Company
www.hachette.co.uk
www.hachettechildrens.co.uk

Queen Aurora's Birthday Surprise

Daisy Meadows

Story One
Three Times the Fun

Story Two
Party Problems

Story Three
Birthday Magic

Aisha and Emily are best friends from Spellford Village. Aisha loves sports, whilst Emily's favourite thing is science. But what both girls enjoy more than anything is visiting Enchanted Valley and helping their unicorn friends, who live there.

Boxie, Bunting and Boo are three very special unicorn foals! The triplets love helping their mum, Canterpop, to make all sorts of celebrations go with a swing.

Everyone loves the magical party decorations from the kitterflies' shop. But when the party goes wrong, it's Minky's own talents that save the day!

Queen Aurora rules over Enchanted Valley and is in charge of friendship; there's nothing more important than her friends. She has a silver crown, and a beautiful coat which can change colour.

Selena is a wicked unicorn who will do anything to become queen of Enchanted Valley. She'll even steal the magical lockets if she has to. She won't give them back until the unicorns crown her queen.

Spellford

Enchanted Valley

Enchanted Cottage
Golden Palace

An Enchanted Valley lies a twinkle away,
Where beautiful unicorns live, laugh and play
You can visit the mermaids, or go for a ride,
So much fun to be had, but dangers can hide!

Your friends need your help – this is how you know:
A keyring lights up with a magical glow.
Whirled off like a dream, you won't want to leave.
Friendship forever, when you truly believe.

Story One

Three Times the Fun

Chapter One
Boxie, Bunting and Boo

"What about a new scarf?" suggested Emily Turner brightly. "Dad lost his scarf, didn't he?"

Emily's mum shook her head. "He bought himself a new one."

Aisha slurped up the last sip of her delicious raspberry smoothie. "I know!

What about a tie?"

"That's a great idea," Emily said. "But we got Dad a tie last year. Didn't we, Mum?"

"I'm afraid so," said Mrs Turner. Her forehead was creased into a worried frown. Emily and Aisha shared an anxious look across Emily's breakfast table. Her dad's birthday was only a week away, and they still hadn't come up with the perfect present!

Aisha got up from her chair and went to the sink to wash her empty glass. Emily felt a jolt of excitement as she noticed that the keyring clipped on to the waistband of Aisha's jeans was glowing! She looked down at her own keyring, which lay on the table. Just like Aisha's keyring, Emily's was shaped like a

unicorn – and it was glowing as well!

Emily took her glass to the sink too. As she turned on the tap, she whispered to Aisha, "Queen Aurora is summoning us!"

Aisha grinned. Both girls knew that the glow meant they were about to return to Enchanted Valley for another adventure with their unicorn friends!

"Mum," said Emily, "please can Aisha and I go to the pond? Maybe a walk will help us think of present ideas."

"Of course," said Mrs Turner. "Just make sure you're back before lunchtime."

Excitement charged through the girls like galloping ponies. They crossed the road and walked up a muddy path towards the Spellford village pond.

"I can't wait to go back to Enchanted Valley!" said Aisha. "I wonder why Queen Aurora needs our help … I hope Selena isn't causing trouble again!"

Enchanted Valley was a secret land full of magical creatures. The unicorns helped take care of the valley, and Queen Aurora ruled over them all with kindness and wisdom. But a horrible unicorn called Selena thought she should be queen instead – and so she kept coming up with wicked plans to take over. So far, Emily and Aisha had managed to stop her, but they knew that Selena was clever and very determined …

Just as they'd hoped, there was no one around to see what was about to happen except for a pair of ducks paddling through the reeds. The girls took out their unicorn keyrings.

"Let's go!" Emily said with a smile.

They touched the keyrings together. At once there was a dazzling flash, like fireworks lighting up the sky. Aisha and Emily felt their feet leave the ground. They floated up, up, up like balloons – and then their feet settled on to soft grass.

The light faded.

In front of them stood Queen Aurora's magnificent golden palace. Its eight turrets, each shaped like a unicorn horn, rose up into a cloudless blue sky. Pink roses grew over the walls, and the air was sweet with their scent. The palace stood on the top of a hillside, and around it lay misty woodlands, meadows of flowers and a river that gleamed silver in the sunshine.

"We're back in Enchanted Valley!" said Aisha. The girls hugged each other with delight.

They looked towards the shimmering moat of water that circled around the palace. Across it lay a wooden drawbridge, which led through the gates. Usually when the girls arrived in

Enchanted Valley, Queen Aurora came trotting across the drawbridge to meet them.

But today the drawbridge was empty.

"That's strange," said Emily. "I wonder if—"

"*Pssssst!*"

Emily and Aisha looked at each other. "What was that?" asked Aisha.

"*Pssssst!*"

"Is someone there?" called Emily.

Then came a giggle, and a voice said, "Over here! Under the willow tree!"

The girls hurried over to a willow tree that grew beside the moat. Its long, trailing branches formed a curtain that dipped into the water. Aisha pushed the branches aside, and she and Emily stepped beneath the tree. The girls gasped.

Standing there was a tall yellow unicorn, with a purple mane and tail and a blue horn. And beside her were three little unicorn foals! One was purple, one was yellow and one was blue.

The foals trotted around the girls, nuzzling against them and whinnying.

The mother unicorn laughed. "My

triplets are very excited about meeting you!" she said to the girls. "We've heard so much about your adventures, you see. My name's Canterpop. Will you tell Emily and Aisha your names?" she asked her foals.

"I'm Boxie," said the purple foal. He dipped his tiny horn in greeting.

The yellow foal reared up on his hind legs, waving his little hooves. "I'm Bunting!"

The smallest foal trotted behind her mother and then leaped out suddenly. "And I'm Boo!" she shouted.

"It's lovely to meet you all," said Aisha.

Bunting cantered around them again, making the locket that hung around his neck jangle. Emily noticed that each of the three foals was wearing a locket, but Canterpop's neck was bare. "Oh!" said Emily. "Where's your locket? Selena hasn't taken it, has she?"

"No," said Canterpop. "Thank goodness! I've lent them to my triplets! I look after everything to do with parties and celebrations in Enchanted Valley, and my lockets are for presents, decorations and surprises. But today I've given them to Boxie, Bunting and Boo. They aren't old enough for their own lockets yet, but—"

"But we've got a plan, haven't we, Mum?" said Boxie. He swished his purple tail excitedly. He wore a locket with a wrapped present in it.

"It's a really good plan!" said Bunting, whose locket contained a big balloon.

Boo looked out from behind

Canterpop. "It's Queen Aurora's birthday tomorrow!" Boo's locket showed streamers streaming and confetti popping.

The girls gasped. They had no idea it was Aurora's birthday!

Canterpop smiled. "Whenever there's a special occasion in Enchanted Valley, I think up the best way to celebrate it. Every year, Queen Aurora tells me she doesn't want a fuss for her birthday – but I know all Aurora's friends would love to celebrate with her. So, triplets," Canterpop said, "will you tell the girls your plan?"

"We're going to throw Aurora a party!" cried Bunting.

"A *surprise* party with lots of amazing surprises!" said Boo. Her eyes shone. "Surprises are the best!"

"And there'll be lots of presents," added Boxie.

"And incredible decorations," said Bunting.

Emily and Aisha grinned. "It sounds brilliant!" said Emily.

"It's why I called you to Enchanted

Valley," explained Canterpop.

"*You* called us here?" asked Aisha.

"Not Queen Aurora?" said Emily.

"Yes!" said Canterpop. "Would you like to help with the party?"

Delight bubbled through the girls like lemonade. "We'd love to!" they said together.

Chapter Two
Party Planning

"Now for the first part of the plan!" said Canterpop. "Wait here, everyone."

Aisha, Emily and the unicorn triplets watched through the branches of the willow tree as Canterpop walked up to the palace drawbridge and tapped her front hoof against the door. "Queen

Aurora?" she called. "Are you there?"

After a little while, a beautiful unicorn trotted out of the palace. As usual, she was a shimmering mix of red, pink, orange and gold – all the colours of a beautiful sunrise. But today, her long

mane was twirled up in curlers and she wore a green dressing gown with a frilly collar draped over her back. It was Queen Aurora! Emily and Aisha smiled at each other – they were always glad to see Enchanted Valley's clever and gentle ruler, but they had never seen her in her dressing gown before!

"Oh, I'm sorry to disturb you, Your Majesty," said Canterpop. "Were you asleep?"

"That's quite all right," said Queen Aurora. Her voice was rich and warm. "I was just styling my mane." Her eyes twinkled. "Let me guess – you've come to ask about my birthday, haven't you?"

Canterpop shook her head. "I know you won't want to celebrate it," she said. "I've actually come to invite you to visit our friend Twinkleangelo with me."

"Twinkleangelo?" Queen Aurora tossed her elegant horn in delight. "I've not seen him for ages!"

Aisha turned to the unicorn triplets, who were pressed up against the girls under the tree. "Who's Twinkleangelo?" she whispered.

"He's a painter," whispered Boxie.

"The best painter in Enchanted Valley," said Bunting.

"And Aurora's friend," added Boo.

Queen Aurora tilted her head thoughtfully. "But I'm not sure I should leave the palace. What if Selena tries another of her wicked plots?"

"No one's seen her for a while now," said Canterpop. "She won't even know you've gone away."

Queen Aurora looked deep in thought for a few moments.

"Please say yes …" Bunting whispered to himself. "Our plan won't work otherwise!"

Then Queen Aurora smiled. "Very well," she said. "Let's go. After all, it would be very, very unlucky for Selena to turn up when I'm away for one night." Her

horn glowed, and golden sparkles swirled around it. Her dressing gown vanished, and then her curlers did too, leaving her mane tumbling around her neck in soft waves. "Now I'm ready," she said. "Off we go!"

Queen Aurora leaped up into the air. Canterpop glanced back at the willow tree to wink at the girls and the triplets, then sprang after her. She and Aurora flew off into the clear blue sky.

"Yippee!" cried Boo. "Now we can set up the surprise party!"

The triplets trotted after Aisha and Emily as they hurried over the drawbridge and into the palace. They retrieved some large bags labelled "PARTY STUFF!" from where they were hidden behind some cherry trees. The girls helped carry them into the palace, through the golden corridors, and into a

huge room the girls had been in before – the Great Hall. It had a gleaming marble floor, statues of important unicorns and a ceiling painted with stars.

Boxie put down the bag he had been tugging along with his mouth. "This is where we're having the party," he

said. He dipped his head into the bag, and pulled out a stack of cards. All of them had "Queen Aurora" written on the envelope. Next he took out presents wrapped in beautiful patterned paper and tied with colourful ribbons. Emily and Aisha helped him arrange them on a nearby table. "All of Queen Aurora's friends send her cards and presents every year," Boxie told the girls. "And this year, they'll get to watch her open them!"

Boo had pulled a heap of envelopes out of her bag. "More birthday cards?" asked Aisha, as she and Emily picked them up.

"Oh no, these are party invitations," said Boo. She waved her horn, and one flew over to Aisha, and another to Emily. The envelopes were a shimmering orange, pink and red – just like Queen

Aurora herself! "Open them," said Boo. Her dark blue eyes were dancing.

The girls tore open the envelopes. Instead of a card, a golden spark flew out of each envelope. Emily and Aisha gasped in amazement as the sparks wrote a message in the air. "*You are invited to Queen Aurora's surprise birthday party!*"

the message said. "*Please come to the Great Hall tomorrow for cake, games and surprises!*"

"Wow!" said Emily. "But how will you send them to all the party guests in time?"

"Like this," said Boo. She ran out of the room and came back wheeling a small cannon. She pulled it over to the open window, then placed the cards inside it. "Off they go," said Boo – and pushed a lever with her hoof to fire the cannon.

BOOM! Both the girls jumped at the noise!

The invitations shot out of the cannon in a shower of gold confetti, then zoomed through the window and flew away.

"That *was* a surprise!" said Aisha with a grin.

Boo giggled. "Surprising people is so much fun!" she said, the streamers in her locket glinting as she spoke.

Bunting was hanging up banners that had a moving picture of Aurora on them, magical flower petal balloons that changed colours and paper lanterns that smelled like strawberries. "So is decorating!" he told the girls. "No party

is complete without decorations. Look, the kitterflies have brought some more!"

"*Kitterflies?*" both girls wondered aloud.

In through the window flew four little kittens. Emily and Aisha could hardly believe their eyes – the kittens had colourful butterfly wings! Their paws and tiny mouths were holding on to banners, bunting and ribbons for hanging balloons and wrapping presents.

"Hello, kitterflies!" Bunting called. Then he turned to Emily and Aisha. "Girls, meet Mew, Mittens, Moggy and Minky. Their parents run a shop called Rippling Ribbons. It's got all the party decorations you can think of. It's my favourite place!"

"Hello, everyone!" mewed Mittens. "We've brought everything you asked, Bunting. Let's set up the net first."

Three of the kittens started to help Bunting hang a net from the ceiling with shiny rainbow ribbons. They tied each ribbon in a beautiful bow to secure the net. "We'll fill the net with colourful

balloons, then when it's party time we'll release the net," explained the foal, "and a hundred balloons will float down. It will be brilliant!"

The girls went to help too. Minky, who was a black and white kitterfly, was trying to tie ribbons to a balloon – but the ribbon got caught around her paws, and she tripped over and landed flat on her fluffy tummy. "Oh, silly sardines!" she squeaked.

Emily ran over and gently lifted her back on to her paws.

"Thank you!" said Minky. Her whiskers drooped. "I wish I was as good at tying ribbons as my brothers and sister – but instead of tying bows, I end up tying knots!"

"We'll help you," promised Aisha.

"We—"

She stopped speaking as the Great Hall suddenly went dark. Through the window, angry grey storm clouds were gathering. A bolt of lightning split the sky as a silvery figure flew towards the palace.

"Oh no," cried Emily. "Selena's coming!"

Chapter Three
A Gift from Selena

With a rumble of thunder that sounded like a hundred beating drums, Selena flew in through the open window. She landed in the centre of the Great Hall, her big hooves ringing on the marble floor. She was tall, and her coat was silver and midnight blue. Her horn was long and looked very sharp. Lightning crackled around it.

The kitterflies squealed with fright, and flew away out of the window. Boxie, Bunting and Boo came to stand bravely beside the girls. Their little legs were quaking.

Selena's eyes flashed as she looked around at the table of presents and cards, the decorations and the invitation cannon. "So, you're having a surprise party for Aurora, are you?" she said. Her voice boomed around the hall. "Where's my invitation, then?"

"You're not invited," Aisha said bravely. "You're not Aurora's friend – you keep trying to steal her crown!"

Selena gave a horrible grin. "Fair point." She jabbed a balloon with her

horn, making it pop. "But even though I'm not invited to your silly party, I've still got Aurora a birthday present."

Selena waved her horn. With a flash of lightning, a large box appeared in front of her. It was decorated with a pattern of a unicorn wearing a crown, but the unicorn wasn't Aurora, it was Selena herself.

Emily eyed it suspiciously. "What is it?"

"We know you won't have bought Aurora something nice," added Aisha.

"Actually, it's a very nice present indeed," said Selena. "Very *unusual.* Very *surprising.*" Her lips curled into a smirk. "If you don't believe me, why don't you take a look for yourselves?"

"I'll look! I love presents!" Boxie trotted up to Selena's gift. With his little purple horn, he lifted the lid off the box. Bunting and Boo trotted over too, and the triplets peered inside.

"Wait, Boxie," said Emily. "It could be a—"

But she was too late. "Surprise!" screeched a voice – and a raccoon leaped out!

The triplets whinnied with shock, and

pranced back to the girls. The raccoon was grey, with a thick, stripy tail. He wore a stripy T-shirt and a black mask was fastened

over his eyes. In his claws was a yo-yo, which he whirled up and down on its string.

Emily frowned. "What sort of present is this, Selena?"

Selena cackled. "I already told you – a surprise …"

Just then, the raccoon flicked his yo-yo at Bunting. It wound around Bunting's locket, then flew back to the raccoon – whisking the locket off Bunting's neck! The girls leaped in front of Boxie and Boo to protect their lockets, but the raccoon's yo-yo shot out twice more and grabbed Boxie's locket, then Boo's. Then he scampered up on to Selena's shoulder.

"Surprised?" asked Selena nastily.

"Our lockets!" wailed the unicorn triplets.

"Give those back, Selena!" Aisha cried.

"I don't think so," Selena snapped. "Change of plan, everyone. This isn't going to be a birthday party any more – it's going to be my coronation party for me becoming queen at last!"

The raccoon was using his yo-yo to snatch balloons and ribbons down from where Bunting had carefully hung them on the walls.

"Well done, Bandit," Selena told him. "You're an excellent thief."

"Sure am," Bandit said. "I'm the best in the business. Nothing's safe around me!"

"Just think," said Selena. "Tomorrow this hall will be full of trolls, witches, ghouls and goblins, all come to celebrate me being queen of Enchanted Valley. It'll be the best party ever!" She turned to

Bandit. "Give me two of those lockets," she told him.

Bandit gave her an elaborate bow. "Here you are, Your Nastiness," he said, and handed them over.

"And you hide that third locket," Selena said. "I know you love stolen things, so

that's your reward for helping me."

"But you promised me a different reward, remember?" Bandit said, his eyes wide.

"Yes, yes," said Selena. "You'll get your fancy new yo-yo as soon as I'm queen."

Bandit grinned delightedly. He scurried off, leaving a trail of stolen balloons and ribbons dragging behind him.

"I'm off to get ready for my party," said Selena. "I need a bath in my giant whirlpool, then I'll find my favourite smoky eyeshadow." She cackled. "I hope Aurora isn't too *surprised* when she finds out what's happened! Ha!" And with a crack of thunder, she flew away through the open window.

"This is terrible!" cried Boxie. "We

wanted to give Queen Aurora a wonderful birthday party … but instead we've lost her kingdom!"

Chapter Four
On Bandit's Trail

"None of this is your fault," Emily told the unicorn triplets. Their eyes had filled with tears and they hung their heads sadly. "It's Selena's and Bandit's!"

"But if we hadn't arranged for Queen Aurora to leave the palace, this never would have happened," said Boo. Her

bottom lip trembled and Aisha gave her a hug.

All around the Great Hall, the decorations were transforming. The "Happy Birthday, Aurora" banners turned into "Congratulations, Queen Selena" banners, with Selena's smirking face on them. The balloons shrivelled like raisins, and the ribbons went limp and fell on the ground.

"We're going to fix this," Emily said. "We'll get the lockets back and put everything right."

"Let's go after the locket Bandit's got first," said Aisha. "Come on – follow that raccoon!"

The ribbons Bandit had been trailing were still slithering out of the door.

The triplets looked a little happier.

They were all hurrying out of the Great Hall, when a pitiful "*Meeeooooow!*" came from under the table piled with cards and presents. Emily and Aisha peered under it – and saw Minky the kitterfly.

"It's all right," Emily told her. She stroked Minky's silky-soft head. "Selena's gone – it's safe to come out now."

"I tried to fly away with my brothers and sister," Minky told them, "but I got tangled up in ribbons again! Look!"

Sure enough, a number of colourful ribbons were caught around her paws and wings.

As the girls untangled

her, Minky said, "I saw that raccoon running off with ribbons trailing behind him. I might not be good at hanging decorations, but I'm very good at chasing ribbons! I can help you catch him!"

"That would be brilliant!" said Aisha, untying a knot of yellow ribbon from Minky's tail.

The trailing ribbon was nearly out of sight. Minky flew after it. "Quickly!" she mewed, and the others followed her.

They all ran through a grand ballroom – where the hoofprint-patterned wallpaper was peeling off the wall – and on through Queen Aurora's art gallery, where a couple of crooked paintings showed dark swamps instead of bright hilltops. A paperweight shaped like a mermaid fell off a desk in the study,

shattering into pieces.

Bunting groaned. "It's all because the Decorations Locket is missing," he said. "Oh, I hate seeing beautiful things ruined!"

The ribbons were wiggling up a winding set of stairs. Minky swooped after them. "Up here, come on!"

They set off up the stairs. Round and round and round they went, climbing higher and higher. The triplets' hooves clip-clopped on the stone steps. Apart from Minky, who fluttered on ahead, everyone was soon out of breath.

"This … is … one of the … turrets … in the corners … of the palace," panted Boxie.

Distant green meadows flashed through the windows. Finally, they reached the top of the turret. It was a small room with paint flaking off the wall. A picture of the palace lay on the ground, broken in two. The room had large windows – and one of them was open …

At the top of the window, Bandit's upside-down face appeared. He grinned cheekily at them, then swung down into the room. Aisha saw he was still holding his yo-yo – but the locket he'd had was gone.

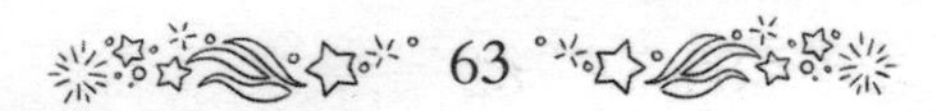

"What have you done with the locket, Bandit?" she demanded.

Bandit sniggered. "Hee! It's somewhere you'll never find it, that's for sure. And even if you did, it's tied up sooooooooo tightly, you'll never get it free. Hee hee!"

He smirked at them and spun his yo-yo up and down.

Emily, Aisha and the unicorn triplets peered out of the window. They looked all around for the locket. Aisha scanned the palace garden and a courtyard filled with fruit trees. "How can we spot something so small from up here?" she muttered.

Emily loved science, and she tried to think scientifically. *Bandit climbed in from the top of the window*, she thought. *As if he was climbing down from somewhere …*

She looked up at the pointed spire

at the top of the turret. Right on its point, something was glinting in the sun …

"There it is!" Emily cried. "I've found it!"

Chapter Five
Minky to the Rescue

Boxie, Bunting, Boo and the girls peered up at the locket gleaming on top of the spire. "That's very high," said Boo in a solemn voice. "How will we get it down?"

"If only Mum was here," said Boxie.

Bunting gave a big sigh. "She could fly us up there."

Boo nodded sadly. "But unicorns can only fly when they get their own magic powers – and we haven't, yet."

"Do you think you could climb up there, Aisha?" Emily asked.

Aisha studied the roof for handholds but couldn't see any. "I don't think so," she said in dismay.

Bandit gave a snort of laughter. "Aren't I a brilliant thief?" he boasted. "It doesn't even matter that you've found the locket – you'll never get it down!"

"I can do it!" said a tiny voice.

Aisha and Emily looked round to see little Minky perched on top of the door. She fluttered her butterfly wings.

"I'll get your locket back," Minky said, and flew out of the window.

"Noooooo!" screeched Bandit. He

leaped up and scampered after her – but Emily and Aisha jumped to stand in front of the window, blocking his path. Bandit stamped his feet. "Let me past!"

Emily glanced at the yo-yo that Bandit was still clutching in his claws. It gave her an idea … "Aisha," she said in a loud whisper, "I don't think Bandit's as good a thief as he thinks he is." She took a coin out of her pocket. "I don't think he'd be able to steal this coin!"

Aisha realised in a flash that Emily was trying to distract Bandit so Minky could rescue the locket.

"You're probably right," she added loudly. "I bet he couldn't."

Bandit growled. "Yes I could!" He stepped closer to Emily and reached a paw out for the coin.

"No, you don't," said Emily, moving the coin behind her back.

While Bandit tried reaching around Emily, Aisha glanced out of the window. Minky was hovering right at the top of the turret! Her little butterfly wings were beating so fast they were a blur, keeping her in place while she tugged at the ribbon holding the locket to the spire with her paws.

"Almost … done …" Minky muttered to herself.

Then, in a rush, the ribbon floated free and draped over Minky's tail. And in her tiny mouth, she caught the locket! Emily grinned up at her.

The little kitterfly fluttered back down. Bandit reached out and snatched the coin just as Minky flew through the window,

and dropped the locket around Bunting's neck.

"Hah! Knew I could get it," he said, at the same time as Aisha cried, "Well done, Minky!"

Bunting reared up on his back hooves with delight. "Thank you, Minky!" he whinnied, while Boxie and Boo cantered around him happily.

Bandit whirled around. "What's happening?" he said, and his eyes went wide.

All around them, the room was going back to normal. The paintwork repaired itself and the pieces of the broken painting came together. In a flash, it was back on the wall where it belonged.

"Decorations everywhere will be fixed, now we've got the locket," said Bunting.

"Hooray! The palace will look lovely again!"

Bandit stamped his feet. "No! This is no good! Just you wait until Selena hears about this ..." He scampered off, his claws rattling as he went down the

winding stairs.

The friends gave a happy cheer.

But Boo looked worried. "Selena's going to be even more horrible now, isn't she?"

"And she's still got the other two lockets," said Boxie. "We can't have Queen Aurora's birthday party unless we

get them back."

"We're going to find them," Aisha said. "We won't give up! Will we, Emily?"

"No way," said Emily. "We'll find those lockets and give Aurora the best party ever!"

Story Two

Party Problems

Chapter One
A Horrible Surprise!

The Great Hall in the golden palace looked lovely once more, with Bunting's balloons and ribbons decorating the walls. But even though they'd got one of the three stolen lockets back, Emily, Aisha and their friends were still very worried.

"This is the closest Selena has ever got

to stealing Queen Aurora's crown," said Aisha.

Emily nodded. "We should go to Twinkleangelo's house to warn her," she said. "She needs to come back so she can stop Selena."

Boxie gave a big sigh. "But Twinkleangelo lives all the way in Watercolour Falls!"

"That's really far from here," added Minky. "By the time we get there, Selena will have crowned herself queen of Enchanted Valley!"

The girls exchanged worried looks. How could they call Aurora home?

"I know!" Boo tossed her blue mane with excitement. "Let's use my invitation cannon!"

"Great idea, Boo!" cried Aisha. She

gave the little unicorn a hug.

A few moments later, they were gathered at the window, around the cannon. Boo moved her little horn like a pen, writing golden words that floated in the air. They said:

Selena at palace! Please come at once!

Aisha fetched an empty envelope from the table that was piled with Aurora's birthday presents and cards. She held it up. Boo dipped her horn, and with a flash of blue sparkles, the message flew inside the envelope. Aisha licked the flap and sealed it. She placed it inside the cannon and Boo pushed the lever with her hoof.

BOOM!

SPLAT!

The unicorn triplets and Minky squealed with shock. Instead of golden

confetti, the cannon fired out orange gunge! Emily rushed to the window – the gunge was splattered over the lawn and the flowerbeds outside.

"Yuck!" cried Aisha. "What a horrible surprise!"

"Did it send the message?" Emily wondered.

The cannon made a noise like a burp – and the envelope plopped out of it and fell on the floor in a puddle of gunge.

"Oh no!" cried Boo in dismay.

Minky's ears pricked up. "What's that noise?" she wondered. She fluttered over to the pile of birthday cards on the table. Emily, Aisha and the unicorn triplets followed. The cards were jiggling about!

Bunting frowned. "What's wrong with them?" he asked.

A tear appeared in one of the envelopes. The paper burst open … and out scuttled lots of purple beetles! They scattered over the table, legs wiggling.

"Eek!" shrieked Minky, and flew up to the ceiling. The unicorn triplets cantered back, whinnying with fright.

"It's OK," Emily told them all. "They won't hurt you." She picked up the envelope the beetles had come from. There was a card tucked inside.

"You're very brave," Minky called down.

"I like beetles," said Emily. "They're amazing! Did you know that some beetles can communicate using vibrations?" Gently, she moved a beetle aside so she could read the card.

Aisha peered over her shoulder. "What does it say?"

"*Dear Queen Aurora*," read Emily. "*You look silly and you stink! Have a horrible birthday!*"

The three little unicorns stamped their feet. "What a mean message!" cried

Boxie in shock.

Minky fluttered down. "I can't believe anyone would write such terrible things to Queen Aurora!" She shook her fluffy little head in disgust.

"Me neither," said Aisha thoughtfully. "It's another horrible surprise, isn't it? It must be because the Surprises Locket has been stolen."

"And the horrible surprises have just started!" yelled a voice.

Everyone turned around. Bandit was crouching beside the invitation cannon – and around his neck was a locket.

"Selena was very cross that you got the Decorations Locket back," Bandit said. "So I'm not going to let you get the others!" He spun the cannon around to face the girls and their friends. "Leave the palace right now – or I'll cover you in gunge!"

Chapter Two
Bandit on the Run

"We're not scared of a bit of gunge!" shouted Aisha. "Do your worst, Bandit!"

Bandit grinned. He adjusted his mask, gripped the cannon's firing lever with both paws – and yanked it.

"Duck, everyone!" Emily cried. She crouched to the ground. Boxie, Bunting and Boo threw themselves down beside her with a clatter of hooves. Minky was fluttering in the air, gaping at the cannon in fright – so Aisha leaped up and caught her, just like a goalkeeper making a save. She dropped down, cradling the trembling kitterfly.

BOOM! went the cannon.

SPLAT! went the stream of orange gunge that shot out of it. The gunge whizzed over the friends' heads and splurted over the wall behind them.

"*YOOOOOOW!*" shrieked Bandit. He scampered out of the hall, his paws clasped tightly over his ears.

"After him!" cried Aisha. "He's got the Surprises Locket!"

She and Emily led the way. Bandit sprinted down a long corridor, ducked into a pretty courtyard with a fountain and sweet-smelling lilac trees, and disappeared back into the palace through a green door. All the while, he kept his paws pressed to his ears.

"That cannon really frightened him," Emily said as they chased after Bandit.

"I think he's scared of loud noises!"

They hurried through the green door too, into the palace kitchens. Inside were rows of worktops and ovens, with pots and pans hanging on the wall. Delicious scents wafted around them.

A pale blue unicorn wearing a chef's hat was stirring a bowl of green mixture.

"Chef Yummytum, have you seen a naughty raccoon?" Boo asked.

"He's stolen our mum's lockets," explained Bunting.

A saucepan fell on the floor with a crash. Aisha glimpsed a streak of grey fur disappearing around one of the cupboards. "There he is!" she cried.

The girls, the unicorn triplets and Minky raced after Bandit. They ran past rows of cookies on cooling racks, and then … *BANG!* A lid burst off a pan, and burnt popcorn flew up into the air. It showered down over the friends.

"*YOOOOOOW!*" Bandit yelled. "More nasty noise!" He put his paws back over his ears, and ran out of one of the kitchen doors.

"Urgh!" grumbled Bunting. "This

popcorn is making my mane sticky!"

"It's another horrible surprise!" said Boo, shaking popcorn from her tail.

Chef Yummytum helped brush them down. "Good luck getting the lockets back," he called, as they followed Bandit out of the kitchen. "And as quickly as possible, please! It's ruining all my cooking!"

Bandit was scampering up a grand staircase with a thick red carpet. Up they went after him. At the top was a large room with crowns and prancing unicorns carved into the walls and ceiling, all painted gold. Rows of glass cabinets displayed beautiful, glittering gemstones – shimmering green emeralds, piercing blue emeralds and dazzling diamonds.

Bandit scurried from cabinet to cabinet,

peering into each one. "Where is it?" he muttered. "Where could it be?"

"What's he looking for?" wondered Boxie.

Emily shook her head. "I don't kno-*oooooooooooow!*" Her words became a yell

– because suddenly the girls and their friends were all falling! The floor beneath them had transformed into a steep slide. They plunged down it, whizzing away into darkness …

Chapter Three
A Mysterious Mess

"This is anoooooooother naaaaaasty surpriiiiiiiiiise!" cried Aisha, as they hurtled down the slide.

She shot out of it, landing on a big sofa. Emily fell beside her. Then came Boxie, Bunting and Boo, and finally little Minky – who landed with her wings folded over her face. She shook them out, and looked around. "Where are we?" she asked.

Emily groaned as she spotted the front door. "Back in the palace entrance hall," she said. "Bandit could be anywhere by now!"

Aisha got up, and helped the unicorn foals to their hooves. "Let's split up," she suggested. "It'll be the quickest way to search the palace."

So Boxie and Bunting galloped away to look in the east wing, Minky and Boo went to search the west wing, and the girls went to search upstairs. "Watch out for more horrible surprises!" Emily called as they all set off.

Aisha and Emily climbed a staircase that wound up the centre of the palace.

The next landing had a view out over Enchanted Valley and was filled with vases of flowers. A door was ajar.

"Maybe Bandit's in there," whispered Emily.

The girls went inside, and found themselves in a beautiful bedroom with walls painted a soft pink. In the centre was a big four-poster bed with yellow sheets. The chest of drawers was orange, and the bedside table was red.

"Sunrise colours," said Emily. "This must be Queen Aurora's bedroom."

Aisha nodded. "But surely she isn't this messy!" she said.

The duvet was rumpled, the pillows were on the floor, and brushes and curlers lay scattered everywhere. The girls peeked through another open door to find Aurora's bathroom. Bottles of bubble bath and shampoo had been knocked over, and were spilling out on to the tiled floor. The towels lay crumpled at their feet.

Through another door was Aurora's walk-in wardrobe. The shelves were empty. Instead, everything lay tangled on the floor – hats, bags, scarves, mane clips

and bows.

"Could the locket's magic have done this?" wondered Aisha.

"I suppose it is a *bit* of a surprise to

find Aurora's room this messy," said Emily, but she didn't sound convinced.

Through the wall, they could hear a scratching sound. Aisha moved a heap of scarves aside so the girls could press their ears up against it and listen.

"Where is it?" they could hear Bandit

saying. "Where's it gone?"

Aisha looked at Emily. "I think Bandit made this mess," she said. "I think he's looking for something."

Emily frowned. "But what could he be looking for?" she wondered. "He's wearing the Surprises Locket, so it can't be that. What's he up to?"

Aisha led the way out of Aurora's bedroom just in time to see Bandit scampering off down the hall. "Whatever it is," she said, "we've got to stop him!"

Chapter Four
The Balloon Drop

"Boxie!" Aisha called. "Bunting, Boo! Minky!"

The girls were back in the palace's entrance hall. The three unicorn foals and the kitterfly came hurrying to meet them. They gathered together beneath a sparkling chandelier.

"Chasing Bandit isn't working," Emily said. The raccoon had slipped away before she and Aisha had even got close. "Let's trick him into coming to us instead."

"Great idea!" said Boo. "But how?"

"Emily and I have thought up a plan," said Aisha. "We know Bandit is looking for something," she explained. "And we know he's scared of loud noises. So if we pretend we've got what he's after, and then make a loud noise …"

"… he'll be so distracted, we can grab the locket," finished Emily. "We'd rather not scare him, but we can't think how else to stop Selena and save Queen Aurora's crown."

"Let's try it!" said Boxie. Then his purple brow creased into a frown. "We just need something that will make a really loud noise …"

Minky fluttered her wings excitedly. "I know what! This way!"

They all followed Minky as she zoomed back to the Great Hall. She

pointed a paw up at the balloons on the ceiling. Dozens of balloons were gathered up in a net, ready to be released.

"If we drop the balloons, then pop them, it will make loads of noise!" Minky said.

"That's a really brilliant plan, Minky!" said Emily. "Now let's go and fetch Bandit …"

They left Boo hiding next to the button

that would release the balloons. The others went back through the palace, up the stairs, and dodged around the puddle of gunge. At last they found the landing filled with flowers that was outside Queen Aurora's bedroom.

"Our voices will echo down the hall and up the stairs," whispered Aisha. "So wherever he is, he should hear us." Then, in a loud voice, she said, "Silly Bandit! He's searching so hard … but we've already found what he's looking for!"

"Exactly," Emily said, very loudly. "Bandit keeps running away, but really he should be chasing us! Ha!"

Boxie, Bunting and Minky laughed too.

"Bandit will never find that … THING!" Boxie said, so loudly he was shouting. "HA HA HA!"

"HA HA HEE!" laughed Bunting and Minky.

Aisha spotted a little black nose appearing around Aurora's bedroom door. *Bandit!* "It's working," she whispered. "Come on!"

They went back to the Great Hall, chuckling as they went. Emily glanced back to see Bandit padding after them. He followed them all the way into the hall and marched right up to the girls. He looked very cross.

Aisha pretended to notice Bandit for the first time. The locket shone against his fur – she could see tiny streamers whizzing around inside. "Oh, hi, Bandit," Aisha said. "What are you doing here?"

"You've got something," said Bandit. "It's mine! It's very important and I want it back right now!"

Emily glanced up. Bandit was standing right underneath the balloon drop!

"Go, Boo!" Emily called.

Boo hit the button with her hoof. The net pulled back and the balloons tumbled down, bobbing around everyone. Bunting and Boxie lowered their little horns, and charged the balloons. *Pop! Pop! Pop!* Minky pounced on them, swatting balloons with her claws. *Pop! Pop! Pop-pop-pop-pop-pop!*

"Eeeeeeeeek!" shrieked Bandit. "Stop it!

Stop it!"

He leaped into the air with fright – and the locket flew off his neck! Aisha kept her eyes fixed on it as it sailed over the balloons. She sprinted after it, cupped her hands together, and jumped up to catch it. "Got it!" she cried.

"Hooray!" cheered Emily.

Bunting, Boxie and Minky stopped bursting the balloons. Boo cantered up to Aisha, who placed the locket around her neck.

Boo grinned. "We did it!" she said.

Chapter Five
The Stolen Yo-yo

"Meanies!" yelled Bandit. His paws were still over his ears. "That was a horrible trick!"

"We're really sorry we scared you," said Emily gently.

"But we didn't have much choice," added Aisha. "We've got to stop Selena!"

Minky fluttered over to Bandit and stretched out her paws. "Would you like a hug?" she asked him.

Before Bandit could reply, the doors swung open. In strode Selena! Her big hooves echoed around the Great Hall. She swished her long tail and held her head high in triumph. "Almost party time now!" she was saying to herself. "Everything's coming together marvellously. The ghouls are going to organise a game of hide-and-shriek, and the witches are bringing Snakes and Ladders, with real snakes ..."

She stopped when she saw the girls. Then her eyes swept over to Boo, and the locket around her neck. Lightning flickered around her horn and her face turned as angry as a storm cloud.

"Bandit!" Selena snapped. "You silly raccoon! You'll never have your yo-yo back now!"

"Look," said Emily. "She's got his yo-yo around her neck!"

It was tied to the third locket, which glinted against Selena's chest. Her horn flashed again, and the yo-yo came loose and rolled along the floor. Bandit started to run towards it, but Selena stopped the yo-yo with her hoof. She bent her horn towards it, and ... *Whoooooosh!*

A lightning bolt struck the yo-yo, which crumbled into ash.

Bandit burst into tears. Emily ran to put her arm around him. "That was a horrible thing to do!" she told Selena crossly.

"So that's why Bandit was helping you," Aisha said. "Because you stole his yo-yo!"

"Th-th-that's right," sobbed Bandit.

"She said if I helped her she'd reward me with a new one, but then I lost the first locket, so she t-t-took away the one I already had. Boo hoo!"

"That's right," said Selena. "No yo-yos for you, Bandit – not until you learn to be a good servant. Now stop that snivelling – it's my party tomorrow! And it's going to be the nastiest, most horrible party ever! Now, time for some sleep. I'm going back to my castle, so don't think you've got any chance of getting this locket. Scary dreams to you all!"

Selena stomped back out of the Great Hall. Bandit wiped his nose and scuttled after her.

"Poor Bandit," said Emily.

Aisha sighed. "I don't think he really wants to help Selena."

They all jumped when the doors opened again – but this time, it was Chef Yummytum! Floating in front of him was a tray laden with bowls of popcorn. The delicious smell of caramel wafted around them. "I thought you could do with a snack!" Yummytum said.

Boo pranced around the hall with happiness. "Now that's a *nice* surprise!" she said. "The magic of the Surprises Locket is working!"

They all tucked into the popcorn. "We still need to find the Presents Locket, though," said Boxie. "We can't get Queen Aurora a special present withoooooouuuuuu …" His words turned into a big yawn.

Aisha glanced at the window. The sky was inky black. "We'll need a good night's sleep if we're going to fix everything before Aurora's party tomorrow," she said. "Come on!"

Before long, they were back in Queen Aurora's bedroom. They'd tidied up the room and Emily and Aisha were tucked up at the top of the bed, while the unicorn triplets lay at the bottom. Minky was right in the middle – she was already asleep, her wings fluttering every time she snored.

Emily snuggled the duvet closer around herself. Both girls knew that no time passed at home while they were in Enchanted Valley, so their parents wouldn't be worried about them. Despite everything, Emily couldn't help smiling – they were having a sleepover at a unicorn palace!

"Good night, everyone," Aisha said softly.

"Good night," the three unicorns said. Minky gave a loud snore.

"We've got a lot to do tomorrow to save the kingdom," Emily murmured, and they all drifted off to sleep.

Story Three

Birthday Magic

Chapter One
Ghastly Gifts

"Paaaaaartyyyyyyy tiiiiiiiiime!"

Aisha rubbed her eyes. Where was she? And who was shouting?

By her feet, three little unicorns stirred – and Aisha remembered! Minky was still curled up in the middle of Queen Aurora's big comfy bed. Beside Aisha,

Emily pushed back the sunshine-yellow duvet.

"Something's happening outside!" Emily said.

The girls hurried to the window. Below, the broad path leading up to the palace gates was packed. Trolls lumbered along, carrying limp, sludge-coloured balloons. A pair of witches carried a cauldron between them, with snakes peering out of the top. A gang of goblins scampered up to the palace, sniggering as they knocked the flowers off the rose bushes they passed. They were all chattering excitedly.

"Selena's guests," said Aisha with a groan. "They're here for her coronation party."

"This is really bad," Emily said. Worry buzzed inside her like an angry wasp. "If

we don't get the last locket back, Selena's going to become queen."

"Let's try sending a message to Aurora again," Aisha said. "Maybe there's something she can do."

Gently, the girls woke Minky and the unicorn triplets. Chef Yummytum had left a tray of toast and jam outside the bedroom door, and they ate it as they ran back to the Great Hall. Aisha and Emily rolled the invitation cannon back to the window, while Boo used her horn to write a message to Queen Aurora:

Selena about to become queen! Please hurry home!

The golden letters hung in the air for a moment, then whooshed inside the envelope Minky had fetched from the table of gifts. Minky dropped it inside the cannon, Boo pushed the lever with her hoof and … *BOOM!* It fired out the envelope in a shower of gold confetti. They watched it zoom away over the palace.

Emily gave a sigh of relief. "It worked! Thank goodness we've got the Surprises Locket back."

But they still needed to get the Presents Locket.

Voices rang from outside the hall. "Bring it in here," one of them said. "I want all my guests to see me sitting on it!"

Aisha's eyes went wide. "Selena!" she said. "Hide, everyone!"

They scrambled under the gift table. The doors opened, and two trolls came in, carrying a beautiful silver throne

decorated with heart-shaped jewels. On it was a red velvet cushion.

"That's Queen Aurora's throne!" Bunting whispered as she scowled.

Selena came in behind the trolls. She had a long purple cloak draped over

her back, and silver ribbons sparkled in her mane. After Selena came more trolls, witches, ghouls and goblins. Soon the Great Hall was thronging with Selena's horrible, noisy guests.

The trolls placed the throne at the end of the hall and Selena jumped up and sat on it. "Music!" she demanded.

Four goblins began to play. One of them played a violin that made an awful screeching sound, another beat a drum out of time, while another whacked at a keyboard that needed tuning. The fourth goblin sang – very badly. "*Oooooh, Queen Selena,*" he wailed. "*How we adore her … She's so much better than Aurora …*"

The witches bopped along to the song while the trolls chuckled as they tore down ribbons and kicked the balloons around the hall. Selena watched them, her lips curled into a smirk.

Under the gift table, Emily nudged Aisha. "Look," she whispered. "Selena isn't wearing the locket any more. I wonder where she's hidden it?"

Selena beat her hoof against the armrest of the throne. "Quiet!" she ordered. With a last screeching note, the band stopped. Everyone fell silent. "I. Want. My. Presents," Selena said. "Now!"

The girls and their friends stayed huddled close together as the guests came up to the table they were hiding under to collect the presents and take them to Selena. Minky scooted back from a pair of big, smelly troll feet, her little nose wrinkling.

One of the witches placed a gift in front of Aurora. She ripped it open with her horn to reveal a perfume bottle filled with grey liquid. "Eau de Anger!" she said. "It's horrible! I love it!"

Next she tore open a gift brought by a goblin. Inside was a book called *Nasty*

Recipes for People You Hate. Selena cackled with delight. "That's everyone!"

Under the table, Boxie's eyes filled with tears. "All Queen Aurora's presents have turned horrible," he whispered. "And they'll stay like that unless we get the locket back."

Selena opened a box of sprout-flavoured chocolates and unwrapped a plant pot filled with thorns. "I've got the

palace," she said, "and I've got a party. Now all I need is the crown. Bandit!" she called. "Come here!"

Bandit scuttled out from behind the goblin band. "Yes, Your Nastiness?"

"I've got one more task for you," said Selena. "If you do it, I'll give you that new yo-yo you wanted."

Bandit's ears pricked up. "Will you really, this time?"

Selena glared at him. "Are you calling me a liar?!"

Bandit hung his head. "No, Your Awfulness. What would you like me to do?"

Selena gave a wicked grin. "When Aurora comes back … I want you to steal the crown from her head!"

Emily and Aisha exchanged horrified

looks. Queen Aurora would be on her way back by now because of them. And she would be walking right into a trap! If they didn't stop Selena, she would soon rule over Enchanted Valley!

Chapter Two
A Clever Trick

The unicorn triplets and Minky leaned in close to the girls. "We've got to find that locket before it's too late," Emily whispered. "I don't think Selena would risk hiding it far away from her. It might even be right here in the hall!"

"Let's search," whispered Aisha. "Be

careful, everyone!"

They crawled out from under the table. Minky fluttered into the corners of the room, checking behind tufted chairs. The three little unicorns darted behind piles of wrapping paper and balloons, while the girls dodged around the statues dotted about the hall. They peered under Selena's horrible presents and looked behind decorations for any sign of the locket.

"*Pssssst!*"

Emily and Aisha looked round to see Boxie beckoning them with a wave of his purple horn. The girls crept over to where he and his siblings were hiding behind a curtain. Minky flew down too.

"I've found the locket!" Boxie told them. His eyes were bright with excitement. "Selena's sitting on it! Look!"

The girls peeked around the curtain. Sure enough, the chain of the Presents Locket was dangling out from under the red velvet cushion on the throne. The band had started playing again, and Selena was tapping her hoof along to the miserable music. She wriggled about, settling deeper into the cushion.

"It doesn't look like she's going to get up any time soon," said Aisha. "We need to make her move somehow!"

Emily glanced at the horrible presents piled around the Great Hall. They gave her an idea …

"Selena loves her horrible gifts, doesn't she?" Emily said. "Maybe we could wrap up something really big, so it can't be carried over to her. Then she'll have

to get up off the throne if she wants to unwrap it."

"Great idea, Emily!" said Aisha. "Maybe one of the statues?"

They all looked around the hall. One of the statues was a serious-looking unicorn, and another was a phoenix with its wings spread out. In the corner was an elf statue with a happy grin on its face. Emily and Aisha spotted it at the same time.

"That one's perfect," said Aisha.

Boo giggled. "Selena will hate it because it's so happy!"

Boxie and Bunting crept over to grab some wrapping paper from the opened presents, while Boo took a roll of sticky tape from the gift table. "I'll help with the ribbons," said Minky. She darted about

the Great Hall, zipping down to snatch pieces of ribbon from the floor.

The girls ducked from window to window, hiding behind the curtains, until they reached the cheerful elf statue. Aisha tore off pieces of tape for Emily to fix the wrapping paper in place. "It just needs your ribbons now, Minky!" Emily whispered.

The little kitterfly flew round and round the statue, tying it up in ribbon – and tying up Aisha too! "Oops!" Minky said. "I'm sorry, Aisha!" But Aisha couldn't help giggling as Boo helped tug the ribbons off her with her horn.

The present was ready. Boxie swished his tail nervously. "I really hope this works," he said.

"Here goes ..." said Aisha. She cupped her hands to her mouth, and shouted, "Selena! You've got another present over here, and it's MASSIVE!"

Selena sniffed. "Bring it here, then."

"We can't!" Emily called. "It's too ENORMOUS!"

But Selena shook her head. "A queen does not leave her throne," she said with a sniff. "Bring it to me – or I don't want it."

Boxie sighed. "We're never going to get

the locket back," he said. Bunting and Boo hung their heads sadly.

Aisha clenched her fists. "We're not giving up," she said. "If Selena won't move on her own, then we'll just have to make her." One of the pieces of ribbon Minky had accidentally tied around her was still caught on her sleeve. Aisha held it up. "And I think I know how ..."

Chapter Three
Stopping Selena

"Oh, snortbags!" exclaimed a troll standing at one of the windows. She jabbed a big green finger at the glass. "It's Aurora! She's coming back!"

Emily and Aisha looked around – and sure enough, they could see Queen Aurora flying through the sky! She shone against the fluffy clouds, as bright as a sunbeam.

"Excellent," said Selena with a smirk. "Bandit! Get ready!"

"Right away, Your Unkindliness," said Bandit, and scurried off.

"We've got to hurry," muttered Aisha.

She grabbed an empty box, and Minky flew inside it – just as they had planned. The unicorn triplets kept watch while Emily quickly covered the box in some toadstool-patterned wrapping paper she'd found on the floor. Before she closed the lid, Emily whispered, "Are you sure about this, Minky?"

Minky nodded, her wings fluttering. "I'd do anything to save Enchanted Valley!"

"You're very brave," Aisha told her.

Emily closed the lid and Aisha tied a

grey ribbon around it. "Here goes," said Emily. She darted across the Great Hall and added the box to a pile of unopened presents near the throne where Selena was still sitting.

The girls and the unicorns huddled in a corner, waiting anxiously.

"Please let her open it," murmured Boxie, jiggling on his hooves. "Please, please, please!"

One of the witches began sorting through the presents. "You've still got lots to open, Your Terribleness," she said to Selena. She held up a small, round present. "How about this one?"

Selena wrinkled her nose. "That's obviously a turnip," she said. "Boring!"

The witch rummaged in the pile. "Maybe this one?" She showed Selena a present with snapping sounds coming from inside.

"That's a Venus flytrap," grumbled Selena. "I've got loads of those."

The witch took off her pointed hat and scratched her head. "What about this present?" And she picked up Minky's box!

Emily and Aisha held their breath as Selena peered at the present.

"I can't tell what that is," said Selena. "I hope it's something really good! Bring it here!"

The witch placed the box by the throne. Selena tore off the ribbon with her horn.

The lid shot up into the air … and Minky flew up out of the box! Selena gave a yelp of horror.

Clutched in Minky's claws was

a big roll of ribbon. She swooped around Selena, zooming as fast as a hummingbird, wrapping the horrible unicorn up in loops of ribbon. In a few moments, Selena's hooves were tied together, and there were so many loops around her body and horn that she couldn't budge!

"Let me go!" shrieked Selena, squirming

on the throne.

The locket dangled out from under the cushion. "Go!" cried Emily, and Aisha started racing towards it. She reached out to grab the locket …

But there was a blur of grey fur in front of her. A paw snatched it up. Bandit's masked face grinned at Aisha. "Told you I was good at stealing things!" he said.

Chapter Four
Thunder and Lightning

"Bandit!" bellowed Selena. "Don't you let go of that locket!"

Bandit scampered over the pile of unopened presents, knocking them flying. He shot through piles of ripped-up wrapping paper and through the legs of the goblin band. The locket was clutched tightly in his paw.

"After him!" cried Emily.

The girls and their friends gave chase. Minky tried to snare him with a loop of ribbon, but Bandit skipped out of the way. Boxie, Bunting and Boo cantered around him in a circle, but Bandit sprang right over Boxie's back. He ran around the Great Hall, Emily and Aisha sprinting after him.

"Keep going, Bandit!" Selena yelled, struggling to free herself from the ribbons. Sparks shot from her horn – and a jet of lightning flashed across the hall, followed by a roar of thunder. It was so loud, the glass in the windows trembled.

"Eek!" cried Bandit. He clapped his paws over his ears. "Horrible loud noise!"

But he kept running. He darted around

a group of witches, and Aisha and Emily hurried after him.

Selena's face was screwed up with fury. "Faster, you silly raccoon!" More lightning lit up the hall, followed by another clap of thunder.

CRAAAAAA-AAA-AAACK!

Bandit pressed his paws even more tightly to his ears. "I hate loud noises," he whimpered.

"Bandit," Emily called, "if Selena becomes queen of Enchanted Valley, it'll always be this noisy!"

Bandit stopped in his tracks. He turned to stare at

the girls. "Really?"

"Really," said Aisha. "There would be thunderstorms every day."

Behind his mask, Bandit's eyes were wide with shock.

The unicorn triplets and Minky caught them up. "If you stop helping Selena, Queen Aurora will stay in charge," said Minky. "She's lovely and quiet. And she would never take your yo-yo."

"Bandit!" Selena yelled. Her voice boomed around the room. "Stop talking to them! Get over here and untie me right now!"

Bandit winced. He looked at Selena, and then he looked at the girls and their friends.

"BANDIT!!!"

Very slowly, Bandit held out the locket

towards the girls.

"Thank you, Bandit," said Aisha. She took the locket and hung it around Boxie's neck. Inside it was a tiny present wrapped in golden paper.

Immediately, the horrible gifts transformed. Selena's pot of thorns became beautiful daffodils, and her *Nasty*

Recipes book became *Tasty Treats*. The Great Hall was filled with lovely things, and the wrapping paper and ribbons that were scattered everywhere had pretty patterns and cheerful colours once more.

"No!" shouted Selena. "This is the worst party ever!" Her horn fizzed with angry sparks.

The hall started to empty. Trolls, witches, goblins and ghouls headed for the doors. "Selena's really cross," muttered a troll. "She's even scarier when she's cross. I'm getting out of here!" All Selena's party guests seemed to agree – in a few moments, they'd gone.

"Good riddance!" Selena yelled after them. "I'm not inviting you lot to any more parties!"

"I think we'd better let her go now,"

said Emily.

They all went over to the throne to untie Selena. The girls unpicked the knots, while the triplets tugged the ribbons away with their horns. Minky had to stop helping, because she was accidentally tying Selena up again! Selena sat fuming while they worked. Emily untied the final ribbon, and as it fell away, Selena sprang to her hooves.

"You may have won this time," she said, "but I will never give up until Enchanted Valley is mine! Next time I'll have such a wickedly brilliant plot, you won't be able to stop me! So there!" Bolts of lightning flickered around Selena, and with a final roll of thunder, she leaped through a window and disappeared into the sky.

The girls and their friends cheered. The

unicorns pranced happily around Emily and Aisha, while Minky flew loop-the-loops around the room. "Hey!" Minky cried, pointing a paw at the window. "Aurora's nearly here!"

They all ran to look. Queen Aurora had landed in the gardens and was striding up the path. Canterpop was on one side of her, and on the other was a rainbow-coloured unicorn wearing a black beret.

"Mum and Twinkleangelo are here too!" cried Bunting.

"And the real party guests are arriving!" called Boo from the other side of the hall. The girls hurried over – through a window they saw a crowd of magical creatures making its way towards the palace, headed by a family of phoenixes and the girls' friend Hob, a little goblin in a purple robe. He was wearing a big bow tie for the occasion.

"We can still give Aurora her birthday party," said Aisha. "But we're going to have to hurry!"

They rushed around the room. Bunting tidied up the decorations and Minky flew up to fix the balloon net, while Boo and Aisha inflated more balloons to fill it. Boxie and Emily quickly wrapped all the lovely presents and stacked them on the table.

The guests started to pour through the doors. "Thank you for coming!" the girls told them, giving each creature a party hat to wear.

Minky had flown to the window to keep watch.

"Aurora's here!" she cried.

"Places, everyone!" called Aisha. The party was about to begin!

Chapter Five
Happy Birthday, Queen Aurora!

"SURPRISE!" everyone yelled as Queen Aurora cantered through the grand double doors.

Aurora gasped. As she looked around at the beautifully decorated Great Hall and the happy crowd of guests, her shocked

expression turned into a delighted smile. “Oh my!” she said. “I was expecting to find Selena here, not a lovely party! This is wonderful!”

"Oh," said Emily, "we just sent you that message to make sure you came home ..."

Aisha winked at her, and Bunting, Boo and Boxie all began to giggle.

"Well, you certainly fooled me!" Queen Aurora said. "What a relief!"

Canterpop and Twinkleangelo followed Aurora into the hall. All the guests started chatting together and eating the surprising treats brought in by Chef Yummytum, which were on trays that magically floated around the room. There were seashell cookies that crunched with the sound of the sea, bowls of soup that changed taste with every spoonful and cupcakes that produced beautiful rainbows when they were bitten into. Twinkleangelo admired the decorations while Canterpop rushed over to her foals and the girls.

"What a splendid party," she said. "I knew you could do it!"

Bandit was sitting in the corner, trying to make a yo-yo out of some ribbon and a burst balloon.

"Poor Bandit," said Emily. The girls, the unicorn triplets and Canterpop went over to him. Boxie waved his horn, and the magic of the Presents Locket transformed the ribbon and balloon into a brand new yo-yo!

"Yay!" cried Bandit. He sent the yo-yo whirling up and down on its string. "This is brilliant – thank you! I'm really sorry I helped Selena," he said, "and for being a thief. I'm not going to do that any more – I'm going to do cool yo-yo tricks to make people happy instead!"

He spun the yo-yo round, and a group of guests came to watch. "How marvellous!" cried Hob, clapping his hands.

Canterpop drew close to her foals and the girls. In a low voice, she said, "From what Bandit said, it sounds like Selena really was here after all!"

"She was," said Boxie.

"She took the lockets," said Boo.

"But we got them back," Bunting said. With shimmering sparkles, the three lockets vanished from the triplets' necks, and reappeared on Canterpop's.

"I'm so proud of you for standing up to that horrible unicorn," Canterpop said.

"Thanks, Mum!" said Boxie. Then he sighed. "But we still haven't got a present for Aurora."

"Ahem," said a voice. Twinkleangelo had appeared beside them. "I couldn't help overhearing," he said. "How about a special portrait of Aurora for her to hang in the hall? Would that be a good present for her?"

"That would be perfect!" said Boxie. "But won't it take ages to do?"

Twinkleangelo winked at them. "Not with magic!"

Soon everyone was gathered together for Twinkleangelo to create his portrait. Rainbow sparkles burst from his horn. First an easel with a canvas on it appeared, then a palette of paints and some brushes, all floating in the air. Twinkleangelo dipped his horn into the paint. The colours swirled in the air, mixing together, then settling on the canvas.

"Done!" Twinkleangelo

declared.

Emily and Aisha went to look – and to their amazement, saw a perfect portrait, as clear as any photograph!

"It's for you, Queen Aurora," said Boxie, a little shyly. "Happy birthday from all

your friends!"

"Thank you so much," Queen Aurora said. "This is the best birthday I've ever had." She smiled at Canterpop. "You were right – parties are fun! Being with everyone I love is the best present of all, and this painting will help me remember the most wonderful day ever."

At last, it was time for the girls to go home. They said goodbye to Canterpop and hugged each of the triplets in turn. "We can't wait to see you again," Boo told them.

"I can't wait either," Queen Aurora told them with a smile. Then, lowering her voice, she added, "I've got a feeling you've done more for me today than throwing this lovely party … Thank you, girls, and see you soon!"

"Goodbye!" said Emily and Aisha, hugging her tightly. "And happy birthday."

Aurora waved her horn and sparkles swirled around the girls. They floated up, up, up ... and then their feet were on firm ground, and they were once again standing beside the pond back in Spellford. The two ducks were still paddling around, quacking to each other.

"What an amazing adventure!" said Aisha with a happy sigh. "Weren't the little triplets sweet?"

"They were," agreed Emily. Then she grinned. "Aisha, it's given me an idea for Dad's birthday present. We can throw him a surprise party. We'll invite all his friends, and it will be the most wonderful day ever, just like Aurora said."

"That's perfect!" cried Aisha. "I'll help you plan it!"

The two girls hurried back to Emily's house, chattering about invitations, balloons – and unicorns!

The End

Join Emily and Aisha
for another adventure in...

Quickhoof and the Golden Cup

Emily Turner and Aisha Khan skipped joyfully ahead of their parents. It was a gloriously sunny day and they couldn't wait to watch the football match! The Spellford Seals were playing their rivals, the Greenlea Gazelles.

The Khans lived in a pretty thatched house in Spellford called Enchanted Cottage. Aisha and Emily had met on the day Aisha moved in and the girls had been best friends ever since. Emily touched the blue and gold striped scarf she wore. "Thanks for lending me a Seals scarf," she said. "I look like a real football fan."

"You soon will be," said Aisha excitedly. "The Seals' best players are Sasha Fry – she's their top striker – and Dena Walton. You should see Dena race down the wing!"

Emily grinned. "I haven't a clue what strikers and wings are, but I'm looking forward to the match," she said. "Who's your favourite player?"

"Bella Bates, the goalkeeper," said Aisha. "I'd love to be able to save goals like she does, but I'm better at passing and scoring."

"I'm no good at any of those things!" Emily sighed. "I can tell a battery clip from a crocodile clip in science, but I'll struggle with football."

"Well, I struggle in science," Aisha laughed. "We could help each other!"

Emily grinned. "Teamwork!"

"Exactly," said Aisha. "It's the team that matters, you don't need to know individual players. The Seals are the best team ever!" She laughed again. "In my opinion, that is."

Mrs Khan handed out tickets as they joined the queue for the turnstile. Emily peered past the line and saw a grandstand on each side of the pitch. As she looked down at her ticket to see where their seats were, a glow of light caught her eye. She drew a sharp breath, and nudged Aisha.

"Your keyring," she whispered.

Aisha glanced down at the crystal unicorn keyring that dangled from her belt. It was glowing!

Emily pulled a keyring from her pocket. "Mine's glowing, too!"

The girls knew what this meant. Queen Aurora was calling them back to Enchanted Valley!

Aisha and Emily had discovered an amazing secret in the attic of Enchanted Cottage – a crystal statuette of a unicorn. When a sunbeam shone on it, the girls were magically carried off to Enchanted Valley, a beautiful land of unicorns and other magical creatures. Aurora, the unicorn queen, had used a spell to create the crystal keyrings after their first adventure together.

The girls' eyes shone with excitement.

"Do you think this means Selena's causing trouble again?" Emily asked.

Selena was a mean unicorn who wanted to take Queen Aurora's crown and rule Enchanted Valley herself.

"If she is," Aisha said grimly, "we'll stop her. We've done it before. Come on!"

They knew that no time would pass while they were in Enchanted Valley. They wouldn't miss the match, and no one would miss them!

The girls ducked behind an ice cream kiosk and held up their keyrings. The crystal unicorns glimmered in the sunshine.

"Ready?" said Emily.

"Ready!"

They felt the keyrings pulling towards each other. When the horns touched, dazzling sparkles swirled around Aisha and Emily – blue, pink, indigo and green. Faster and faster the sparkles whirled, lifting the girls right off the ground! They laughed with excitement as Emily's long hair whipped around her head. As they touched down and the sparkles started to fade, the girls knew that in a moment, they would see Queen Aurora's glittering golden palace sitting on a lush green hilltop, overlooking peaceful meadows and gently bubbling streams.

"Oops, look out!" An imp wearing running shoes leaped to one side to avoid crashing into Emily.

"Coming through!" cried a little bunny, turning a series of flips.

The girls looked around them. Although they were in front of the palace, the usually peaceful grassy slopes were crowded with unicorns and magical creatures, all running, jumping, skipping or doing gymnastics. The air was filled with excited squeals and laughter. Unicorns trotted in and out of the palace, carrying baskets of bunting, banners and balloons.

On the hillside beyond was a huge stadium of gleaming silver.

Emily's mouth dropped open. "That wasn't here last time," she said.

The stadium's delicate walls looked as if they'd been woven from strands of silvery candy floss. Flags of every colour fluttered high above on long, twisting, silver poles.

"Cool!" Aisha gasped. "I think something sporty's happening!"

Emily grinned. "Definitely!" She pointed to the sky, where their friend Fluffy the cloud puppy was playing a game. It looked like rugby, except that his ball was a small grey raincloud. Other cloud creatures chased him, until a cloud bunny caught him and grabbed the fleecy ball. Fluffy rolled on his back and lay giggling in the air.

The cloud bunny flicked the ball with her puff of a tail. It floated down towards an elderly pixie on the ground below. The cloud bounced once, gently, on his head, then began raining on him. His eyes widened in surprise.

Aisha giggled. "It's a cloudburst!"

They headed for the palace, passing a team of gnomes in swimming trunks marching towards the moat. Chuckling pixies practising broomstick racing whizzed overhead, and a great beating of wings made the girls look up. They waved to a tumble of dragons, who were having a flying upside down race.

Near the palace, the girls spotted their mermaid friends shrieking with laughter as they played water polo in the crystal-clear moat. The mermaids waved.

"Everyone's gone sport mad!" said Aisha, waving back.

A unicorn came out of the palace and trotted lightly over the silver drawbridge. Her mane and tail were glossy gold and her coat shimmered with the pearly colours of a summer dawn: pink, orange, yellow and red.

"Aurora!" cried Emily.

The unicorn queen wore a silver crown, and her horn gleamed gold. Around her neck hung a locket with two tiny golden suns dancing around each other. All the unicorns in Enchanted Valley wore magical lockets. Aurora's was the

Friendship locket. While she wore it, her magic made sure that Enchanted Valley remained peaceful and friendly.

"Welcome, girls!" Queen Aurora said in her soft, lilting voice. "I'm so happy you came. We're getting ready for the Enchanted Valley Games!"

"It looks exciting!" said Emily.

"What's going to happen?" asked Aisha.

Aurora's golden mane sparkled. "Once every four years we have lots of different sports and fun games," she said. "This evening, at sunset, we're having a grand opening ceremony. I thought you'd like to join us."

"We'd love to!" Emily said. "It looks like the sports here are a bit different from the ones we play at home."

Aurora smiled. "Some are, but there'll also be lots you know."

Hoofbeats pounded, and four unicorns cantered over the hillside towards them.

"Here are the Sports and Games Unicorns," said Aurora. "They'll be judges and referees, and they'll make sure everything goes well."

The girls noticed that, as well as lockets, all four wore golden whistles around their necks.

Aurora introduced them. "Quickhoof takes care of Teamwork," she said.

A unicorn with a buttercup-yellow coat dipped her horn to say hello. Her chestnut mane and tail matched her soft brown eyes. Her locket had a medal inside it.

"Hello, Quickhoof," said the girls.

"Brightblaze is in charge of Confidence," Aurora continued, as a pearly-coloured unicorn with a scarlet mane and tail dipped her horn in greeting. Her locket was the same colour as her mane and had a twinkling golden trophy inside.

"Fairtail sees to Sportsmanship." A sea-green unicorn lowered her horn, and as she got up they could see her locket – a rosette of darkest blue.

"And Spiritmane looks after Perseverance."

A lavender unicorn with a creamy mane and tail greeted the girls. Her locket held a bright white scroll. She was smiling but then her smile suddenly dropped and she stared over Emily's shoulder.

The girls turned to see a small greeny-brown whirlwind moving swiftly across the meadow.

Also available

Book One:

Book Three:

Daisy Meadows

Unicorn Magic

Glitterhoof's Secret Garden

From the author of RAINBOW MAGIC

Book Four:

Book Five:
Daisy Meadows
Unicorn Magic
Silvermane Saves the Stars
From the author of
RAINBOW MAGIC
Book Six:
Daisy Meadows
Unicorn Magic
Dreamspell's Special Wish
From the author of
RAINBOW MAGIC
Book Seven:
Daisy Meadows
Unicorn Magic
Slumbertail & the Sleep Pixies
From the author of
RAINBOW MAGIC
Book Eight:
Daisy Meadows
Unicorn Magic
Brighteye & the Blue Moon
From the author of
RAINBOW MAGIC

Book Nine:
Daisy Meadows
Unicorn Magic
Quickhoof and the Golden Cup
from the author of RAINBOW MAGIC
Book Ten:
Daisy Meadows
Unicorn Magic
Brightblaze Makes a Splash
from the author of RAINBOW MAGIC
Book Eleven:
Daisy Meadows
Unicorn Magic
Fairtail & the Perfect Puzzle
from the author of RAINBOW MAGIC
Book Twelve:
Daisy Meadows
Unicorn Magic
Spiritmane & the Hidden Magic
from the author of RAINBOW MAGIC

Special One: Special Two: